The Berenstain Bears®
All in the Family

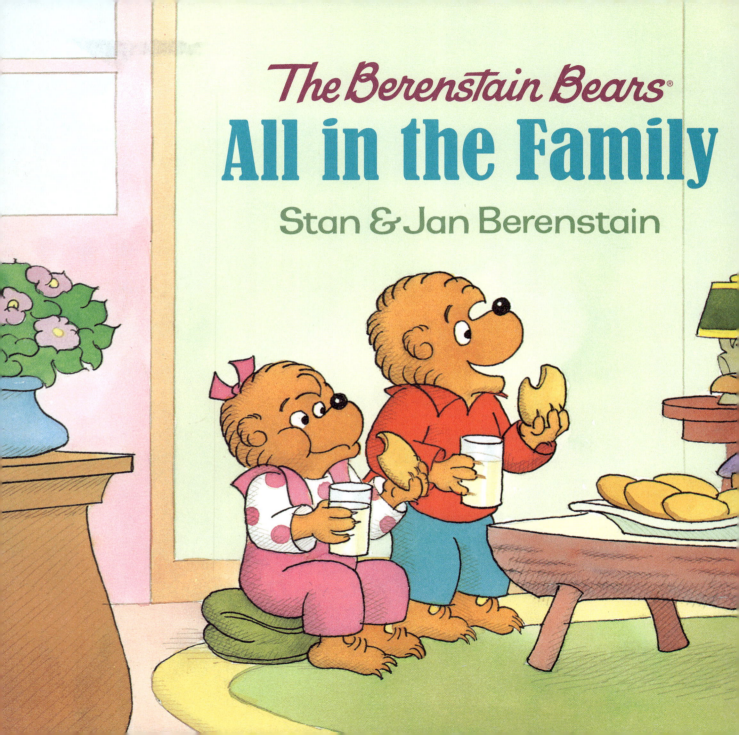

Random House 🏠 New York

All rights reserved. Published in the United States by Random House
Children's Books, a division of Random House, Inc., New York.

The stories in this collection were originally published separately in
the United States by Random House Children's Books as the following:

The Berenstain Bears and the Week at Grandma's
copyright © 1986 by Berenstain Enterprises, Inc.

The Berenstain Bears and the Trouble with Grownups
copyright © 1992 by Berenstain Enterprises, Inc.

The Birds, the Bees, and the Berenstain Bears
copyright © 2000 by Berenstain Enterprises, Inc.

The Berenstain Bears and Baby Makes Five
copyright © 2000 by Berenstain Enterprises, Inc.

The Berenstain Bears and the Papa's Day Surprise
copyright © 2003 by Berenstain Enterprises, Inc.

The Berenstain Bears and the Mama's Day Surprise
copyright © 2004 by Berenstain Enterprises, Inc.

Random House and the colophon are registered trademarks
of Random House, Inc.

Visit us on the Web!
randomhouse.com/kids
BerenstainBears.com

Educators and librarians, for a variety of teaching tools, visit us at
randomhouse.com/teachers

ISBN: 978-0-307-93068-2
Library of Congress Control Number: 2011925430

MANUFACTURED IN CHINA   10 9 8 7 6 5 4 3 2 1   First Edition

Contents

The Berenstain Bears
and the
WEEK AT GRANDMA'S

When mama and papa bears
go away,
Cubs visit their grandparents
for their first long stay.

A FIRST TIME BOOK®

Once in a while the Bear family, who lived in the big tree house down a sunny dirt road deep in Bear Country, got out the family snapshots and looked at them.

"What are these?" asked Sister Bear, picking up a book of photos. "I don't think I've ever seen these before."

There were pictures of bears playing tennis, canoeing, dancing, and having all sorts of fun. The bears looked like Mama and Papa, only they were younger and thinner.

"They're pictures of Papa and me on our honeymoon," said Mama with a smile.

"At Grizzly Mountain Lodge," said Papa. "We had a wonderful time!"

"What's a honeymoon?" asked Brother.

"A honeymoon is a special trip couples take when they get married," explained Mama. "Getting married is a very special happening, and celebrating it with a trip is an old custom."

"As a matter of fact," said Papa, "we've decided to go on a *second* honeymoon. We're going back to the same place and play tennis, go canoeing, and have fun!"

"It'll be lovely," said Mama.

13

"A second honeymoon sounds like a pretty good idea to me," said Brother.

"Me, too," said Sister. They scooted out of the room and were back in a jiffy with their vacation things.

"Oh, you won't be coming," said Papa. "Honeymoons, even second honeymoons, are just for grownups, not for cubs."

"But . . . but what's going to happen to us?" asked Sister.

"It just so happens," said Mama, "that Gran has been after me to let you spend a week with her and Gramps. And this will be the perfect opportunity."
"A whole week?" said Brother.

"But we've never stayed with anybody that long!" said Sister.

"Well," said Papa, taking a few practice swings with his tennis racket, "there's got to be a first time for everything."

"What will we do for a whole week?" asked the cubs. "Where will we sleep? What will we eat?"

"Goodness!" said Mama. "Such a fuss about a simple thing like spending a week at Grandma's."

It didn't seem like a simple thing to the cubs. They loved Gramps and Gran very much, but . . . well, they just weren't Mama and Papa.

Besides, Gramps and Gran were sort of . . . *old.*

"What are you taking with you?" Sister asked Brother when it was time to pack. "I'm taking two books, my jacks, and my teddy, of course."

"These," he said, holding up some books and his best yo-yo.

Papa put their suitcases in the car trunk last so that when they got to Gran's, unloading was as easy as one-two-three.

Then, after lots of big bear hugs and kisses, the happy second honeymooners were on their way.

"It certainly is good to see young folks having fun," said Gran as she waved good-bye.

"*We're* the young folks," muttered the cubs. "*We're* the ones who are supposed to have fun."

"I'm sure you're hungry after your ride," said Gran when they went in. "How about some of my special honey nut cookies and milk?"

"No thanks, Gran," said Sister. "I'm not hungry right now."

"Hey, these are really good," said Brother.

Sister sneaked a taste. They *were* good, but . . . well, they just weren't Mama's.

"Now let's get you up to your room so you can get settled," said Gramps.

The cubs reached for their bags, but before you could say "Grizzly Gramps," they were gathered up, bags and all, and carried up the steep stairs. Gramps certainly was strong for someone so . . . *old*.

The room at the top of the stairs was very nice—very nice, indeed, but . . . well, it just wasn't home.

"Gramps," said Sister, "where do you suppose Mama and Papa are right now?"

"Well," said Gramps, "I reckon they're still on the road, just pulling into sight of Grizzly Mountain Lodge."

After they unpacked their things, Gramps thought the cubs might like to explore around the house.

While it wasn't home, it *was* an interesting house. There was the attic crowded with all *sorts* of interesting things . . .

Gran's kitchen with its yummy tastes and smells . . .

and Gramps' den. Gramps knew how to build a ship in a bottle. When the cubs asked him how it was done, he just smiled.

"What do you suppose Mama and Papa are doing now?" they asked then.

"I reckon they've gotten into their tennis clothes and are swatting the ball back and forth," he said.

Over the next few days Brother and Sister found lots to do. They helped Gran feed her bird friends—more kinds than they had ever seen in one place. And Gran knew all their names.

They helped Gramps cut and smooth twigs for a new ship in a bottle. It turned out that he built them *outside* the bottle and then slid them in. It was pretty tricky.

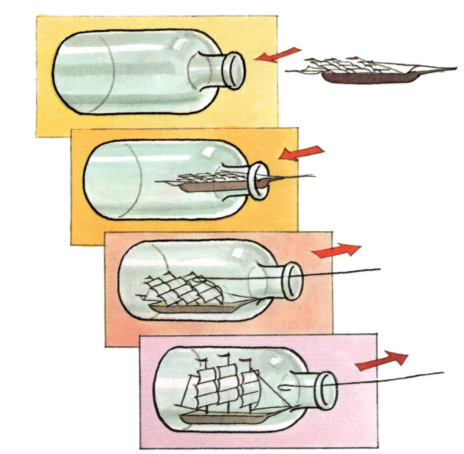

They went fishing in a special place Gramps knew about.

"Well," said Gramps as they returned with a fine catch, "I reckon that your mama and papa are out canoeing right now."

"I certainly hope they're having fun!" said Sister. "Because we sure are!"

"Hmm. Better get these chairs in,"
said Gramps after a fine fish fry.
"It's going to rain tomorrow."
"How do you know?" asked Brother.
"I can feel it in my bones,"
answered Gramps.

It turned out Gramps was right.

"Good," said Brother. "We'll be able to relax a little." Sister got out her jacks and he started to play with his yo-yo.

"Used to be pretty good with one of those myself," said Gramps.

Was he ever! Not only could Gramps make the yo-yo sleep and walk-the-dog, he could even do baby-in-the-cradle and round-the-world!

That evening, after a refreshing nap, they all went to Gramps and Gran's regular Friday night square dance. Gramps and Gran didn't just watch. They do-si-doed with the best of them. They even won a prize—for Friskiest Couple.

"Goodness!" said Sister in the morning. "This week really flew by!"

"And we learned so much," added Brother, practicing baby-in-the-cradle.

"Gramps and Gran, how come you know so much?" asked Sister. "So many things! Why, you can even feel the weather in your bones!"

"That's one of the good things about being an older person," said Gramps, smiling. "You learn something every day. So that by the time you're old enough to be a grandparent, you know quite a lot."

"Gee," said Sister, "I guess you and Gran are so old you must know *everything*!"

"Oh, no," said Gramps, laughing. "You never stop learning. Why, just this week we learned something very special. We learned how absolutely wonderful it is to be grandparents and have lovely grandcubs."

Then Gramps and Gran swept their grandcubs up in a big hug.

The next thing they knew, a familiar *beep! beep!* was heard. It was Papa tooting the horn. He and Mama were back from their second honeymoon and it was time for the cubs to go home.

After saying good-byes and thank-yous, the Bear family piled into the car and headed home. No sooner were they on their way than Brother and Sister were bubbling over with the fun and excitement of their week at Grandma's.

"Well," said Papa, "sounds like you had a pretty good time."

"Oh, we *did*!" said Sister. "Papa, sometime you might want to go on a *third* honeymoon. Then we could spend another week at Grandma's."

"A *third* honeymoon?" said Papa. "I don't think anyone's ever gone on a *third* honeymoon."

"Well," said Sister, "there has to be a first time for everything!"

The Berenstain Bears
and the
TROUBLE WITH GROWNUPS

Grownups and cubs
get quite a surprise
when they see themselves
through the others' eyes.

A First Time Book®

Even though it was bright and clear outside the Bear family's tree house, there was a storm brewing inside. For while it would be wrong to say that cubs and grownups are natural enemies, it would be fair to say that cubs and grownups sometimes don't get along.

"Where's the rest of my paper?" thundered an angry Papa Bear, storming into the living room. It didn't take him long to find Brother Bear and the sports section.

"I just borrowed it," said Brother. Papa snatched it up and plumped down in his easy chair. Brother wandered into the kitchen looking for sympathy from Mama Bear. "Gee," he said, "what's eating him?"

"Your father looks forward to his evening paper," Mama said, "and he has a perfect right to be annoyed when half of it is missing—and furthermore, I'll thank you not to refer to your father as *him*!" She stomped out of the kitchen.

"Why not? He's a *him*, isn't he? Gosh," said Brother, "what's eating *her*?"

What was "eating" Mama was Sister Bear. Sister had been on the phone with Lizzy Bruin for almost an hour.

"But Mama!" she protested when she was told to say good-bye.

"Don't 'But Mama' me!" said Mama Bear. "This is not your private phone. You've had all day to talk to Lizzy at school, and you'll have all day to talk to her tomorrow. *So hang up that phone now!*"

Sister did as she was told.

Later, at dinner, Brother and Sister got into a little more trouble. "Peas and mashed potatoes again," said Brother under his breath.

"And what," Papa asked, "is wrong with peas and mashed potatoes?"

Brother was about to answer that they'd had them three days in a row, but he thought better of it.

Instead, he began counting and spearing peas onto his fork, "One—two—three—four . . ."

"What are you doing?" asked Sis.

"Trying to see how many peas I can get onto my fork at one time," he answered.

45

While Brother was counting peas, Sister was working on her mashed potatoes. She patted them into a little mountain, and then using her spoon, she pressed a cup in the top. "Pour it right there," she said when Mama offered her gravy.

"What in the world?" commented Mama.

"Well, you see," said Sister, "it's a volcano, and the gravy is going to be the lava and flow down the sides."

"That will be quite enough of volcanoes and counting peas!" shouted Mama. "Food is to eat, not to play with!"

"Gee whiz," said Brother. "We're just trying to make it interesting."

"Food isn't supposed to be interesting!" roared Papa. "It's supposed to be food!"

47

Brother and Sister went to bed that night and got up the next morning without much fuss. But trouble started again at breakfast.

"Oh yes," Brother said, suddenly remembering something. "We'll be getting the late bus home this afternoon because—"

"Late bus?" interrupted Mama. "I was planning on our visiting Gran after school."

"But Mama," he protested, "we're staying late to plan for the Parents Night Talent Show next Friday."

"Parents Night?" she said. "First I heard of it."

"And Friday is my chess night with Farmer Ben," complained Papa.

"Here's a notice I brought home," said Sis, digging into her bag. "I forgot to give it to you."

"Me too," muttered Brother.

"Why, this notice is a week old!" said Mama.

"Forgot? Forgot?" roared Papa. "Why, you cubs would forget your heads if they weren't attached to your shoulders!"

"Phew!" breathed Brother as he fell into the seat beside Cousin Fred on the school bus.

"Tough morning?" asked Fred.

"You better believe it!" said Sister, taking the seat Lizzy had saved for her.

The four compared notes on the way to school. The cubs agreed that while there was no doubt that their parents loved them, they were a little difficult to get along with sometimes. They nagged; they said *no* a lot; and they never wanted cubs to have any fun.

"Hey," said Brother as they got off the bus, "what are we going to do for the Parents Night Talent Show?"

"Don't know," said Lizzy. "Let's think about it."

That afternoon the auditorium was filled with cubs getting ready for the show. Babs Bruno was playing her violin. Queenie McBear was practicing pirouettes. Too-Tall and his gang were working on a rap number, which Teacher Bob didn't look too happy about. Brother, Sis, Fred, and Lizzy didn't have an idea yet.

But as they searched their brains, Brother snapped his fingers and said, "I've got it! Remember what we were talking about on the bus this morning?"

"Sure," said Fred. "We were saying how grownups can be a big pain."

"Well," said Brother, "let's put on a play about that, and call it . . ."

"The Trouble with Grownups!" shouted all the others. "Sensational!" said Sister as they slapped hands, delighted with the idea of showing parents how hard it is being a cub.

53

But putting on a play is easier said than done. You have to write it, figure out who is going to play the parts, then memorize it. Then you have to worry about costumes and scenery. The cubs did all that. It was hard, but it was fun, and they did it all in secret. Costumes for Fred and Lizzy were easy. They were going to be Brother and Sister, so they just borrowed their extra clothes. Getting costumes for Brother and Sister wasn't so simple, because they would be playing their own mama and papa.

They managed by letting Gran in on the secret. She was a wizard on the sewing machine, and she made them great-looking little Mama and Papa costumes. The four practiced their parts, and before they knew it, it was time for the big Parents Night Talent Show.

There was a lot of talent at the Bear Country School, and all the acts did pretty well, but it was Brother, Sister, Fred, and Lizzy's play that was the hit of the show.

The audience of parents laughed and laughed when they saw how they seemed to their cubs. Mama laughed until tears rolled down her cheeks. Papa laughed, too, but not as much as Mama.

They both thought the play, which was a big surprise to them, was very well done. They admitted that it helped them understand what it was like being a cub.

59

The next morning Mama and Papa had a bit of a surprise for their cubs. You might even say a shock.

Mama, who was a sewing wizard herself, had made a grownup-size pink jumper. Wearing it, she looked like a huge Sister Bear. She even had a pink bow. Papa, wearing a red pajama top and blue bottoms, looked like a gigantic Brother Bear. The cubs were confused.

"It's very simple," explained Mama. "You helped us understand what it's like being cubs. By pretending we're the cubs and you're the grownups, we're going to show you what it's like being parents."

Before Brother and Sister could say a word, Mama and Papa began acting like cubs.

"Where's breakfast? I'm hungry!" shouted Papa.

"I hope we're not having that gooey oatmeal again!" screamed Mama.

"Ooey gooey oatmeal! Ooey gooey oatmeal!" shouted Papa, jumping up and down.

Brother pulled Sister into the living room, where they could hear themselves talk. But the living room was another shock. There were things all over the floor. Not toys, which they sometimes left lying about, but strange things like the vacuum cleaner, Mama's sewing basket, Papa's chain saw, and his wrench set. What a mess!

The cubs understood. Mama and Papa were showing them what it was like having to pick up after them. Mama and Papa ran through the mess and headed for the front door. Brother cried, "Please don't bang the . . ."

But it was too late. Papa banged the door so hard it shook the house.

Brother began to smile. Sister began to giggle. They went out on the stoop. There were "cubs" Mama and Papa sporting about on the lawn—Mama jumping rope, Papa trying kick turns on Brother's skateboard.

But their feet got tangled, and they sprawled head over heels on the grass. Pretty soon they were all laughing so hard their sides ached.

Later, when they were back to being themselves, Papa said, "I have a better idea how cubs feel now." Mama agreed. Brother and Sister admitted they had a better idea how parents feel, too. "Boy!" said Brother. "You two sure know how to act like cubs!"

"After all, we were cubs once ourselves," said Mama. "And here's a thought: You'll be grownups someday and each probably have cubs of your own."

Brother and Sister thought about that for a moment. They looked at each other. Then they looked off into the distance and thought about it. It was something to think about.

THE BIRDS,
THE BEES,
and the
BERENSTAIN BEARS

When a mama bear's lap
slowly disappears,
she has some special news
to tell her little dears.

A First Time Book®

Sister Bear was a very busy young cub. She liked all different kinds of things. She liked to watch the clouds go by. She liked the color pink. She certainly liked her dolls. She had three of them: a rag doll, a Kewpie doll, and a baby doll that opened and closed her eyes and said, "Mama!"

Sister liked to do all kinds of different things.
She liked to run and jump and climb.

She liked to jump rope.

She liked to ride her trike.

Sister wondered about all different kinds of things. She wondered why the sky was blue. She wondered why the stars twinkled. She wondered what made the wind blow. She reminded herself to ask Papa about those things.

One day when Mama took
her up onto her lap to read a
book, Sister wondered why
Mama's lap was
getting smaller.

"Mama," she said. "Your lap is getting smaller."

"That's true," said Mama.

"Why is that?" asked Sister.

"Why do you suppose?" said Mama.

"Maybe it's because you're eating too much," said Sister.

Mama laughed and said, "I certainly hope not. No, the answer is that I'm going to have a baby."

Sister could accept that.

"Oh," she said. "Mama?"
"Yes, dear," said Mama.
"Aren't you going to read
the book?" said Sister.
"Yes," said Mama. She
read the book.

"When are you going to have a baby?" asked Sister a couple of days later.

"Not for many months," said Mama. "You see, the baby is very small now. It's growing in a special place in my body."

"What kind of special place?" asked Sister.

"It's called a 'womb,'" said Mama.

Sister thought about that. "That sounds like 'room,'" she said.

"*Sounds* like, but *isn't* like," said Mama. "It's a special place that all mamas have where babies can start and grow."

Sister could accept that.

A few days later, Sister was playing with her dolls when Mama walked by.

"How's it going to get out?" asked Sister.

"How is *what* going to get out?" asked Mama.

"The baby," said Sister.

"That's a good question," said Mama. "I'm just about to leave for my appointment with Dr. Gert. Why don't you come along and ask her? She's very good at answering questions."

"Okay," said Sister. "Oh, Brother, would you like to come along?"

"No thanks," said Brother, who was in the middle of making a model airplane. "I went through that before you were born."

Sister could accept that.

"Hello, Sister," said Dr. Gert. "I'm glad to see you. As you know, your mama is going to have another baby. I'm especially glad to see you because I delivered you and your brother."

"Where did you deliver us to?" asked Sister.

"Oh, that's just an expression doctors use for how we help mamas have babies," said Dr. Gert.

DRESSING ROOM

"Would you like to come with us? I'm going to have a look and see how the baby's doing."

"How are you going to do that?" asked Sister.

"We have special machines that let us look inside," said the doctor. "One is called an x-ray machine." Sister knew about x-rays. She had her ankle x-rayed once to see if it was broken. But it was just a sprain.

"This one is called an ultrasound machine," said Dr. Gert as she passed a thing that looked like a TV remote over Mama's tummy. The thing was connected to a big machine that had a little screen. Fuzzy pictures came on the screen. They didn't look much like a baby to Sister. But they must have to Dr. Gert because she kept saying, "Good. Fine. Excellent."

"Your mama said you had a question for me," said Dr. Gert as they were about to leave.

"Yes," said Sister. "How does the baby get out?"

"When the baby and the mama are ready," explained Dr. Gert, "the baby comes down through a part of the mama's body called the birth canal."

Sister could accept that. She couldn't quite picture it, but she trusted Dr. Gert and she accepted it.

"What a beautiful spring morning," said Mama as they walked home through the meadow. The meadow was very lively that day. A pair of robins were feeding their babies. A baby bunny hopped across their path.

"Look!" said Mama, pointing to a deer at the edge of the woods. "See how fat her sides are. She and I might have our babies at the same time."

"Look!" said Sister. "There's one with antlers. Do you think maybe he's the daddy?"

"I think maybe he is," said Mama.

"Gee," said Sister. "It looks like babies, babies all over the place!"

"Looks like," said Mama. "I guess you've noticed all the bees visiting the flowers." How could Sister have helped noticing? The buzz of the busy hovering bees filled the air.

"Does that have to do with babies, too?" asked Sister.

"In a way it does," said Mama. "I guess you've noticed that birds and bears and bunnies and deer all come in males and females."

"Yes," said Sister. She remembered from when she and Brother were very little and used to take baths together.

"Well," said Mama, "it's not just birds and bears that come in males and females. Some trees and flowers do, too."

"You mean there are boy and girl trees and flowers?"

"More like male and female," said Mama. "But that's the general idea. And while the honeybees are gathering nectar to make honey, they're doing another important job. They're picking up pollen from the male flowers and carrying it to the female flowers. It's the female flowers that make the seeds that grow into more flowers."

Sister could accept that.

Spring grew into summer and summer grew into autumn, and Mama grew to such a size that she had no lap at all.

Then one morning she said to Papa, "I think it's time." Papa called up Mrs. Grizzle, the cubs' regular sitter. She came over to stay with Sister and Brother while Papa took Mama to the hospital, where Dr. Gert would help Mama have the baby.

It wasn't long before the phone rang. It was Papa. Mrs. Grizzle answered it. Then she put Sister and Brother on the phone. "The new baby has arrived!" said Papa. "And mother and baby are doing fine!"

"Is it a girl or boy?" asked Sister. "Papa—" But Papa had hung up. Sister turned to Mrs. Grizzle. "He didn't say whether it was a girl or boy."

"Well," said Mrs. Grizzle, "he's pretty excited right now. He just forgot. Besides," she continued, "the important thing is that they're both doing fine."

Sure, that was important, but other things were important, too: like whether it was a girl or boy. And what about a name for the new baby? Sister was hoping for a sister that she could play dolls and stuff with. Brother, on the other hand, wanted a brother to make model airplanes and stuff with.

But while it was true that the new baby wouldn't be able to do any of those things for some time, it could already do quite a lot.

As they found out later that day, it could cry and squirm and wiggle and wet and even hold on to your finger. Someday it would be able to do all the things Sister and Brother could do.

Sister could accept that.

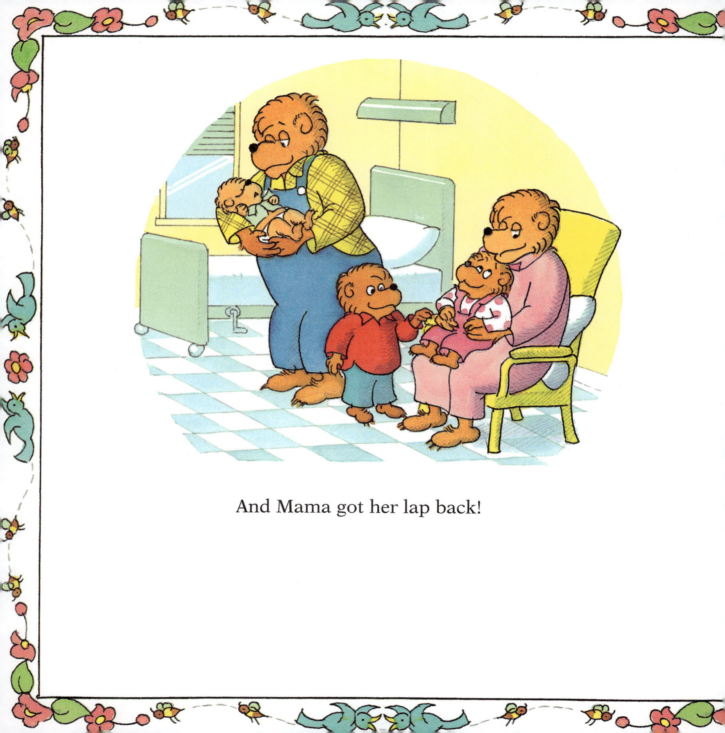

And Mama got her lap back!

The Berenstain Bears
and
Baby Makes Five

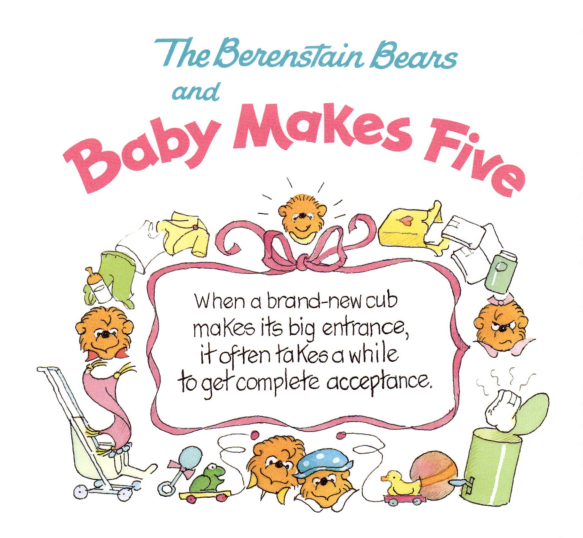

When a brand-new cub
makes its big entrance,
it often takes a while
to get complete acceptance.

A First Time Book®

Big news in Bear Country!

DYDIES

The Bear family, who lives in the big tree house down a sunny dirt road, has a new member: a baby girl named Honey. What fun! What excitement!

What a nuisance!

Sometimes it seemed that it was

crying,

feeding,

burping,

spitting up,

and diapering around the clock.

102

And when it wasn't those things, it was

cuddling,   dandling,

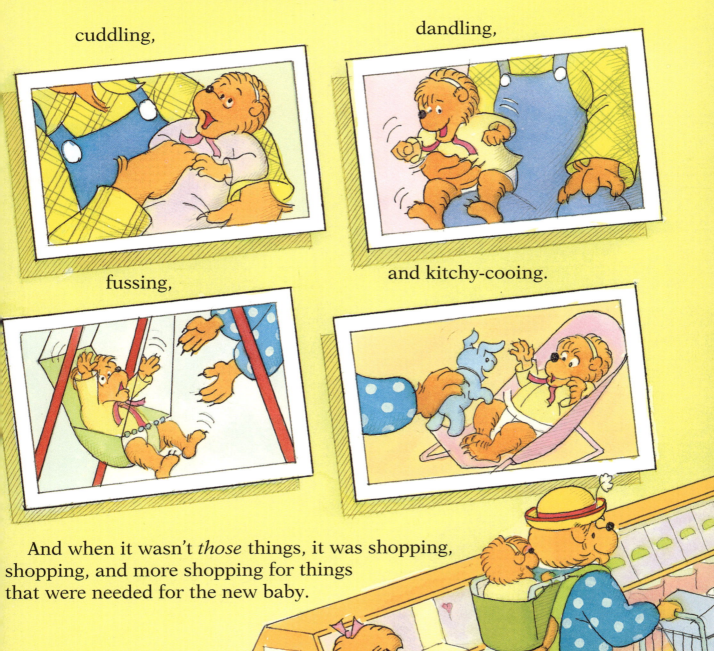

and kitchy-cooing.

fussing,

And when it wasn't *those* things, it was shopping, shopping, and more shopping for things that were needed for the new baby.

At least that's how it seemed to Sister Bear.

Brother Bear understood that babies need
a lot of attention. He'd been through it before
when Sister was born. But having a new baby in
the house was a new experience for Sister, and
she wasn't enjoying it very much.

It didn't help that when Papa came home from work every day, the first thing he did was pick up the new baby, make goo-goo eyes, and say, "How's my darlin' little dumpling?"

Dumpling. Good name for her, thought Sister—a fat little doughball that was hard to swallow.

It didn't help at all when Aunt Min and Uncle Louie visited and made a big fuss over the new baby.

"Well, Sis," said Uncle Louie, "I guess you're not the big star around here anymore. Ha-ha-ha!"

Ha-ha-ha, indeed!

It wasn't just Aunt Min and Uncle Louie. It was as if every bear for miles around came to admire the new baby and say how cute she was!

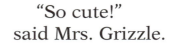

"So cute!"
said Mrs. Grizzle.

"Cute as a button!"
said Farmer Ben.

"Cute as a bug!" said Mrs. Bruin.

"Yeah," snapped Sister under her breath, "a *stink* bug!"

Sister had a point about the new baby being a stink bug. While she couldn't do much, she sure was good at wetting and filling diapers.

"Sister, dear," said Mama one day when she was attending to the baby, "it's not very polite to say 'pee-yoo' every time you come near the baby. Meanwhile, would you do me a favor and slosh this diaper in the toilet before you throw it away?"

"Pee-yoo!"

And the fuss they made when
the baby did the least little thing.

"Get out the tape recorder!
The baby said 'Goo'!"

"Get out the videocam!
The baby is smiling!"

"Call the newspapers!
The baby laughed out loud!"

GOO!

HEH!
HEH!
HEH!

It was easy to see that Sister was getting grumpier and grumpier. At least, it would have been easy to see if Mama and Papa hadn't been so busy with the new baby.

But since babies can't do much for themselves, they do need a lot of care and attention.

113

Brother needed a lot of care and attention when he was a baby. So did Sister. That's the way it is with babies.

It takes Mother and Father Bluebird practically all day digging worms to feed their wide-mouthed babies.

Mother Fox works from dawn to dusk to care for and protect her kits.

Mother Kangaroo carries her joey around in her pouch until it's big enough to do proper kangaroo jumps.

Brother could tell that Sister was seriously out of sorts. She was even angry at her dolls because they reminded her of the new baby. But he had problems of his own at the time—like long division and multiplication tables.

Speaking of school, it was an assignment Sister brought home from school that told Mama that Sister wasn't exactly thrilled about the baby. Teacher Jane had asked each cub in the class to draw a picture of his or her family. Sister liked to draw. She was a very good artist.

This is what the picture looked like:

My Family

Mama Papa Brother Sister

When Mama saw it, she knew there was trouble afoot. "Dear," she asked, "why didn't you put your new baby sister in the picture?"

"Because," snarled Sister, "there wasn't enough room on the paper!" Then she stomped up the stairs, went into her room, and slammed the door.

Oh, dear!

That evening after the new baby was asleep, Mama had an idea. "I know what," she said. "Let's look at our videocam movies."

"Let's not and say we did," said Sister, thinking they would be the latest new baby videos.

VIDEOS: SISTER AS A BABY

But she couldn't have been more wrong. While that's what they looked like, that's not what they were. They were videos that Mama and Papa had taken of Sister when *she* was a baby.

They showed Papa playing kitchy-coo with her. They showed her smiling, laughing, and saying "Goo." They showed her jumping up and down in her Jumping Jack. They showed her doing all the things her new baby sister was doing.

"Will you excuse me a minute?" Sister said when the last video had ended.

"I suppose so," said Mama as she watched Sister scurry up the stairs and into her room.

"What do you think?"
asked Mama.
"I think we'd better go see
what she's up to," said Papa.

Mama, Papa, and Brother sneaked up the stairs to see what Sister was up to. What she was up to was drawing another picture of the Bear family.

This is what it looked like:

My Family

Mama   Papa   Brother Sister   Honey

Mama, Papa, and Brother breathed
a sigh of relief. "It's just about bedtime,
dear," said Mama. "We may as well start
getting ready for bed."

"Mama," said Sister, "could we take a
peek at the baby first?"

"I don't see why not," said Mama.

The Bear family tiptoed very quietly into the baby's room. Sister peeked through the bars of the crib at her sleeping baby sister.

"You know something?" she whispered.
"She *is* kind of cute."

The Berenstain Bears
and the
PAPA'S DAY
SURPRISE

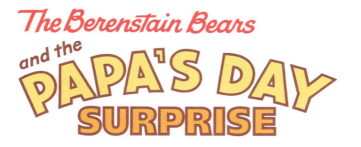

Some papa bears are
embarrassed by sentiment
and pretend not to want
a Father's Day present.

A First Time Book®

Papa Bear is a bear of many opinions. He has opinions about all sorts of things. He has an opinion about the best way to fell trees.

TIMBER-R-R!

He has an opinion about predicting the weather.

THE BEST WAY TO PREDICT THE WEATHER IS BY OBSERVING THE LENGTH OF THE WOOLLY BEAR CATERPILLAR'S COAT.

He has an opinion about the best kind of honey.

NO QUESTION ABOUT IT, WILD, WILD HONEY IS THE BEST!

And though in his opinion, Mother's Day is a fine and proper holiday and a worthy tribute to the institution of motherhood, he didn't think much of Father's Day.

"That's fine with us," said Mama. "It's a busy time for me with the quilting bee coming up. And with the school year ending, the cubs are going to be pretty busy, too."

"Then it's agreed," said Papa. "We are not going to make a fuss about Father's Day."

A few days later, Papa was fixing a creaky front step, Mama was working on her tulip bed, and Baby Honey Bear was playing on the grass. Above their heads a pair of robins was hard at work building a nest.

"The fuss about Father's Day is a lot of nonsense," said Papa. "Look at that daddy robin helping that mama robin build a nest. He doesn't need to have a fuss made over him. He's happy to do his job building the nest, sitting on the eggs when the time comes, and digging up worms when the chicks hatch. That daddy robin doesn't need a special day, and neither do I."

"Yes, dear," said Mama.

Papa was about to continue when he heard a noise in his shop. "Hey," he said, "there's somebody rooting around in my shop. If it's those pesky raccoons again, I'll . . ."

But it wasn't raccoons. It was Brother and Sister Bear.

"What are you two up to?" asked Papa.

"Er—we're just getting some stuff for a school project," said Brother.

"Er, that's right," said Sister, "a school project." Brother was holding a piece of the special paper that Papa used for his furniture designs. Sister was holding a roll of the paper Papa put down when he was painting.

"Okay," said Papa. "Just so it's got nothing to do with Father's Day. Is that clear?"

"Very clear," said the cubs.

But as Father's Day drew closer, talk about it was very much in the air—and *on* the air as well:

on the radio,

AND NOW, WITH FATHER'S DAY APPROACHING, A WORD OF TRIBUTE TO ALL YOU DADS OUT THERE

138

on television,

at the mall,

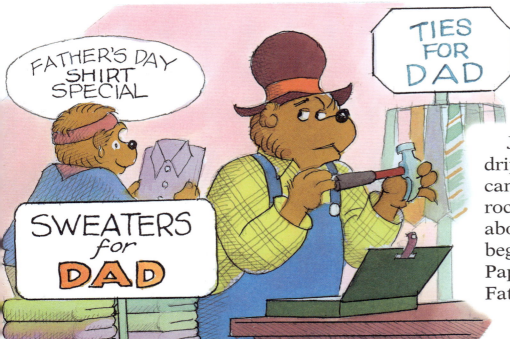

and just about everywhere else.

Just as the drip, drip, drip of water can wear away solid rock, the constant talk about Father's Day began to wear away Papa's opinion about Father's Day.

139

A couple of days before Father's Day, Mama and Papa were in the living room. Mama was putting the finishing touches on a quilt.

"You know," said Papa, "I think maybe I'm being a little selfish about Father's Day. It's a lot of nonsense, of course. But cubs are cubs, and if they want to make a little fuss about it . . ."

"Sorry, dear," said Mama. "I was counting stitches and didn't hear a word you were saying."

Then the phone rang and Mama picked it up. "Yes," she said, "this is she. Yes, Mrs. Bruin. It's all arranged. See you there. Goodbye."

"What was *that* about?" asked Papa.

"Er—just some quilting business," said Mama.

"By the way," said Papa, "where *are* the cubs?"

"They're over at Cousin Fred's working on a big scout project," said Mama.

"Oh," said Papa. "I thought they were working on a big *school* project."

"Er—that's right," said Mama. "It's a big school *and* scout project."

Papa would never have admitted it, but he was beginning to hope that Mama and the cubs wouldn't worry about his opinion regarding Father's Day. He even looked in drawers and closets for hidden presents.

But there weren't any.

Now it was the day before Father's Day. Papa was on his way to his shop when he noticed the daddy robin. Mama robin had laid the eggs and the daddy was sitting on them.

"Mr. Robin," said Papa, "I think Mama and the cubs are up to something. And I think I know what it is: It's Father's Day! They're going to surprise me."

Mr. Robin didn't say anything. He just sat there.

Papa knew what Mama and the cubs were doing. They were *pretending* to skip Father's Day. Well, two could play at that game. Tomorrow morning, when he woke up to breakfast in bed and lots of presents and cards on Father's Day, he would pretend to be surprised.

But the next morning he didn't have to pretend. He really *was* surprised! There was no breakfast in bed! There were no gifts and cards!

But wait a minute! What was that delicious smell coming up from the kitchen? It was his favorite food: French-fried honeycomb. There *was* going to be a Father's Day breakfast. It just wasn't going to be in bed.

But the French-fried honeycomb wasn't for him at all. Mama explained that it was a gift for the new family down the road.

Papa went out and sat on the front steps. The daddy robin flew by. He was carrying a worm to his newly hatched chicks.

"Happy Father's Day, Mr. Robin," said Papa. "For all the good it's going to do us."

145

At that moment Mama and the cubs came down the front steps.

"Where are you going?" asked Papa. "What about breakfast?"

"We're all going for brunch at the Grizzmore Grille."

"Huh?" said Papa.

"The Grizzmore Grille, please," said the cubs as they piled into the car.

When they arrived, folks were lined up at the entrance.
"Look!" said Papa. "There's a sign over the door that says, 'Welcome, Dads'!"
"So there is!" said Mama with a big grin.

147

There was a much bigger sign inside. It said, *"Welcome to the Papa's Day Surprise."* It was painted on the roll of paper the cubs had gotten for the "school project." And there was a stage with a long table.

"Go ahead, Papa," said the cubs. "Up on the stage with the other papas."

He found a chair with his name on it at the long table. Other papas were on the stage with him: Lizzy Bruin's papa, Cousin Fred's papa, even Too-Tall's papa. Other papas filled the seats. And the food! All Papa's favorites: French-fried honeycomb, honey-cured salmon, honeyed squash.

Someone began to speak. It was Mayor Honeypot. "And now we shall hear from those who put this wonderful surprise together. Our first speakers will be Brother and Sister Bear."

Brother and Sister cleared their throats
and read a poem. It was on the special
paper they had taken from Papa's shop.

To the best Papa Bear
in the whole wide world:
You are big and strong and true.
And no matter what we do,
we know we can depend on you.
You cheer us on when we are glad.
You cheer us up when we are sad.
You are always there for us,
to help, advise, and care for us.
Happy Father's Day!

Papa looked out over the audience. But he could hardly see. His eyes were misty and he had a lump in his throat as big as a cantaloupe. After Brother and Sister read their poem, it was Lizzy Bruin's turn to say something about her dad. After Lizzy came Cousin Fred. As the cubs read their tributes, Papa thought about all the wonderful moments he had shared with his family. Well, they weren't always wonderful. But they certainly were moments.

Suddenly there was the sound of applause and cheering. It brought Papa back to the here and now of the Papa's Day Surprise. Cubs and mamas were on their feet. It had been a wonderful party and a wonderful Father's Day!

The guests headed for their homes.

"Cubs," said Papa as he drove down the hill to their tree-house home, "I want to thank you for that lovely poem."

"Mama helped us with it," said Brother.

"Also," said Papa, "I want to thank you for the Papa's Day Surprise. It was a wonderful gift."

"That," said Sister, "was a gift for *all* the papas. We and Mama have a special gift just for you."

"Just for me?" said Papa. He pulled to a stop at the tree house. He hurried up the front steps, through the front door, and into the living room.

When he saw what was waiting for
him, he could hardly believe his eyes.
"A Bearcalounger!" he cried.
"Just what I've always wanted!"
It was a special chair that
you could adjust up and
down. It was the perfect
chair for Papa.

Baby Honey began to
cry. She was hungry.

It was *also* the perfect place to feed Baby Honey.
Mama and the cubs watched with big smiles as
Papa sat back in his new Bearcalounger and gave Baby
Honey her bottle.

The Berenstain Bears
and the
MAMA'S DAY
SURPRISE

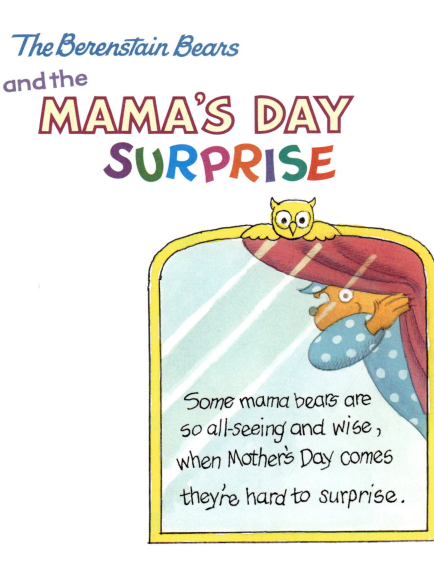

Some mama bears are
so all-seeing and wise,
when Mother's Day comes
they're hard to surprise.

A First Time Book®

Mother's Day was coming, and Mama Bear knew that Papa and the cubs were going to surprise her with a special celebration.

Last year they took her out for a special Mother's Day dinner.

Mama was pretty sure that this year they were going to surprise her with a special Mother's Day breakfast in bed. And alas, she also knew that she would probably have to spend the rest of Mother's Day cleaning up the mess they made preparing her special breakfast in bed. But that was okay. It's the thought that counts.

The signs of Papa and the cubs' Mother's Day plan weren't hard to read.

There was a marker in the cookbook at the page for Mama's favorite breakfast: Honeyed French Toast with Blueberries.

And one day when they were shopping at
the Beartown Mart, she saw the cubs slip off
in the direction of the card department.

As Mother's Day drew closer, Mama knew
that she had a lot to do if her family's Mother's
Day surprise was going to be a success.

163

First, she had to find the old bed tray they used when a family member was ill. She found it at the top of one of the kitchen cabinets where she kept jars and bottles that were too nice to throw away. It had some oatmeal on it from when Papa had been in bed with a cold. She scraped off the oatmeal and put the bed tray where she knew Papa and the cubs could find it.

But there was more to do. She had to make sure they would have the ingredients to make her special Mother's Day surprise. She checked the recipe in the cookbook. Honeyed French Toast with Blueberries called for honey, bread, eggs, sweet cream, sweet butter, powdered sugar, and blueberries. It was Papa and the cubs' favorite breakfast, too. But that was okay. It's the thought that counts. As for the mess they would make in the kitchen—well, that just came with being a mama.

Mama checked the cupboard. There was honey, of course, and plenty of bread.

There was powdered sugar, too. But it was all caked up like a rock.

They were out of eggs. But that wouldn't be a problem. She could get farm-fresh eggs from Farmer Ben. Nor would sweet cream, sweet butter, and powdered sugar be a problem. She would get those at the supermarket. But fresh blueberries? It was much too early in the season for blueberries.

The cubs were with Mama on her next trip to the supermarket. She didn't want to spoil their surprise, so she gave them a little shopping list to take care of while she put sweet cream, sweet butter, and powdered sugar into her cart.

She also bought some extra cleanser and scouring pads for the big Mother's Day clean-up.

She looked high and low for blueberries, but there were none to be found. It turned out that Gran had frozen some last season. That took care of the blueberries.

Mama was also pretty sure that a new bathrobe was going to be part of her Mother's Day surprise. She caught the cubs checking the size of her old threadbare one. But she pretended not to notice. As the big day drew closer, Mama made sure to stay out of the way when she thought they might be wrapping presents.

Finally it was the night before the morning of the big surprise. Papa and the cubs were doing their best not to let on that anything the least bit special was happening. But their secret smiles gave them away.

"Now, here's the plan," said Papa while Mama was off putting baby Honey Bear to bed. "I'm setting my wristwatch alarm for five o'clock in the morning. I'll set the alarm low so it won't wake Mama.

"Then I'll slip out of bed and come wake you two, and we'll sneak downstairs to the kitchen. Now, it's going to be very dark, so we'll have to be careful not to bump into things or we'll wake Mama."

Mama pretended to be asleep when Papa's alarm went off. She lay perfectly still as Papa slipped out of bed.

There was a certain amount of bumping and thumping as Papa and the cubs stumbled around in the dark. Papa even slipped and almost fell down the stairs, but the cubs caught him.

Mama lay awake getting ready to be surprised. But it wasn't easy. From the sound of it, things didn't seem to be going well down in the kitchen. The sound of an eggbeater was to be expected. But then there was a big clunk. What happened? Oh, dear. It wouldn't be the first time Papa dropped the bowl while he was beating eggs.

And what was that burnt smell? They must have burnt the toast.

Mama could just picture the mess they were making in the kitchen. It was all she could do to stay in bed. But after a few more clunks and some muffled shouts, she slipped out of bed, put on her old bathrobe, and stole downstairs to sneak a look at the kitchen.

It was the worst kitchen mess she had ever seen. The bowl had broken, so there was broken crockery and egg all over the floor. There was burnt toast on the drainboard and sticky honey handprints on the walls.

Oh, dear, thought Mama, *it's going to take me a week to clean up the mess. Thank goodness Mother's Day comes just once a year.*

But out of the wreckage
of broken crockery, spilled
eggs, burnt toast, and sticky
honey, Papa and the cubs
had managed to put together
a beautiful breakfast tray of
Mama's favorites:

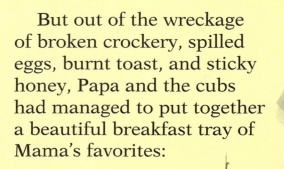

honeyed French toast with blueberries, sassafras tea, and even a small vase of red roses.

Mama sighed. It was so beautiful that it was almost worth the terrible mess they had made.

But now they were coming
out of the kitchen and heading
for the stairs. Mama had to
get out of there or the whole
surprise would be ruined.
She scurried up the stairs
and climbed back into bed.

She pretended to be just waking up when they came into the room with her breakfast tray.

"Happy Mother's Day!" said Brother and Sister.

"Happy Mother's Day, my dear," said Papa as he placed the tray on the bed and plumped the pillow behind Mama's back.

"Mother's Day?" said Mama. "Well, I suppose it is! How lovely! All my favorites: honeyed French toast with blueberries and sassafras tea and these beautiful roses. And look! Just what I needed!" she said as she unwrapped the new bathrobe.

"This is absolutely delicious!" said Mama as she ate her French toast and sipped her sassafras tea. "I don't know how to thank you."

Just then they heard baby Honey Bear's cry of *"Mama! Mama!"*

"I'd better get Honey Bear up and give her breakfast," said Mama.

"No," said Papa. "This is Mother's Day. You just stay in bed and read your cards. The cubs and I will take care of everything."

And they did.

When Mama got downstairs to go to work on the kitchen, she got a *real* surprise. It was the cleanest, shiniest, spick-and-spannest kitchen she had ever seen.

"Well," said Sister, "how did you like your Mama's Day surprise?"

"Yes," said Brother. "How did you like it?" Honey Bear gurgled and Papa beamed.

"How did I like it?" she said. "It was the most wonderful surprise any mama ever had!"

Then she gave her cubs
a great big Mama Bear hug.

All About the Berenstains

Many years ago, when their two sons were beginning to read, Stan and Jan Berenstain created the endearing bear clan that shares their own family name.

Since the first book appeared in the 1960s, they have written and illustrated more than three hundred Berenstain Bears books in a dozen formats, but the most enduring are the stories in the groundbreaking First Time Books® series. These humorous, warmhearted tales of a growing family (the books started with one cub and ended up with three) deal with issues common to all families with children: sibling rivalry, friendship, school, visits to the doctor and dentist, holiday celebrations, time spent together and apart, competition, good manners, and many more.

Each First Time Book® presents a problem that's resolved—usually by Mama and Papa, but sometimes by Brother and Sister—with good sense and, above all, a sense of humor. Lessons are learned and values explained and passed to the next generation, always through the telling of a good story. The Berenstain Bears First Time Books® have sold millions of copies, a testament to their enduring appeal, to the fact that families everywhere can see themselves in the Berenstain Bears—and to the truth that a well-told tale is indeed timeless.